WHERE'S M HOMEWORK?

By Michael Garland

Cartwheel Books
an imprint of Scholastic Inc.

Copyright © 2014 by Michael Garland.

All rights reserved. Published by Scholastic Inc. SCHOLASTIC, CARTWHEEL BOOKS, and associated logos are trademarks and/or registered trademarks of Scholastic Inc.

Library of Congress Cataloging-in-Publication Data available.

ISBN 978-0-545-43655-7

10 9 8 7 6 5 4 3 2 1   13 14 15 16 17/0

Printed in the U.S.A. 40
This edition first printing, January 2014

I looked on my desk.
Nothing!

I looked under the bed.
Nothing!

I looked in the bathtub.
Nothing!

Maybe my sister had seen my homework?
"No, I haven't," she said. "Are you sure you did it?"

"Yes! I did it!"

But where could my homework be?

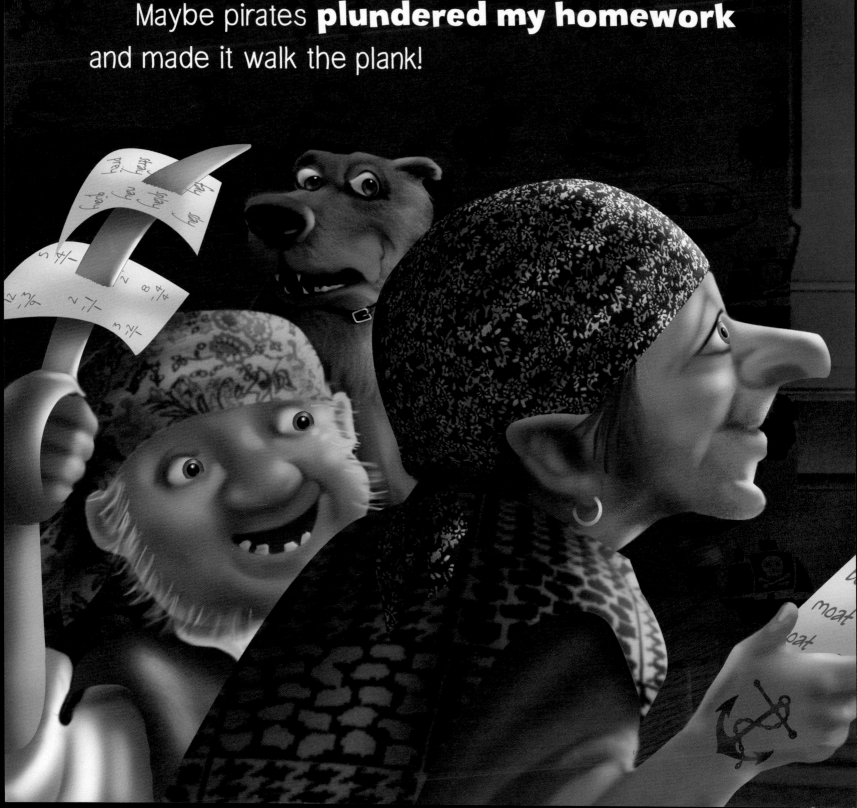

Maybe pirates **plundered my homework**
and made it walk the plank!

Maybe a **big fat boa constrictor** slithered away with it!

Maybe my homework ran away and joined the **circus!**

Maybe a **wicked witch** cast a spell on my homework and turned it into a **frog!**

Maybe a **dragon flew** into my room and **toasted** my homework?

Maybe some wild monkeys climbed in my window and **trashed my homework!**

Suddenly my mother called from downstairs,
"Hurry up, sweetie. You're running late."

Oh, no!
What could I do?

Then, from the living room, I heard something strange. Chewing and licking and slobbering sounds.

It was Frumpy, gobbling up the last pages . . . of **my homework!**

Frumpy looked at me with a big smile as if to say, **"Thanks! That was delicious!"**

I didn't know what else to do, so I took Frumpy to school to explain what happened to my homework.

My teacher looked at Frumpy with one eyebrow raised and said, "Hmmm. So, the **dog** ate your homework?"

But before I could say anything, Frumpy's stomach grumbled. Then came another louder rumble. Frumpy groaned like a volcano that was about to **erupt!**

He tried to hold it in, but it was no use! **Frumpy let it loose!**

"Good dog, Frumpy!"